THE GREAT
BIG
BOOK
OF READING
KINDERGARTEN

Copyright © QED Publishing, 2008

QED Publishing
A Quarto Group Company
226 City Road
London EC1V 2TT
www.qed-publishing.co.uk

ISBN 978 1 84835 208 7

Publisher Steve Evans
Creative Director Zeta Davies

Printed and bound in China

THE GREAT
BIG
BOOK
OF READING
KINDERGARTEN

mjf
media

Contents

The Great Big Friend Hunt

Hannah Ray

Illustrated by Jacqueline East

Henry was a puppy.
A very small, very scruffy puppy.

He lived on a farm with Cleo the cat. Cleo was sleepy.
She never wanted to play with Henry.
Henry got very bored playing by himself.

When Henry was bored,
bad things seemed to happen.

And most of these happened
to poor Cleo!

10

"Oh, Henry," she sighed. "What you need is a friend. That would stop you from being bored."

Henry thought this sounded great. There was just one problem —what was a friend?

Henry headed into the yard where the other animals lived.
He stood up, straight and tall—as straight and as tall as
a small, scruffy dog can. In a loud voice he said,
 "I am going on a Friend Hunt.
A Great BIG Friend Hunt.
Will any of you help me?"

Doug Donkey raised his head.
"Hee-haw! I'll help you, Henry,"
he said.

"Me, too," snorted Peggy the pig.

"And me!" mooed Clara the cow.

Henry was very happy with
all this help. But there was still one
problem—none of the other animals
knew what a friend was either!

Doug Donkey decided to ask his daddy, who was very wise.

"A friend," said Doug's daddy, "is someone to talk to."

Doug Donkey trotted off right
away to tell Henry.

"Oh, thank you!" said Henry. "I'm so glad
you told me! Now we've found that out,
let's keep looking for a friend."

But they couldn't find one, and Henry
was starting to feel really disappointed.

Peggy asked her sister Petunia, who was
very smart, if she knew what a friend was.

"Of course I do," replied Petunia.
"A friend cheers you up when you are sad."

"There you go!' exclaimed Peggy.
"Now we know even more about
friends. I'm sure we'll find one
soon. Chin up, Henry."

Henry felt much better.

But the animals
still couldn't find a
friend. Henry was
beginning to worry
that the day was
almost over.

Clara's cousin, Courtney, had come to stay. She knew so much about so many things. When Clara asked her what a friend was, she answered, "A friend is always happy to help."

With this in mind, the animals hunted high and low—but it was no use. They still couldn't find a friend... and it was starting to get dark.

"Don't worry, Henry," said Clara. "We'll help you look again tomorrow. And the day after that!"

"Oh, Cleo," sniffed Henry when they returned home. "We've hunted all day. We know a friend is someone to talk to. We know a friend cheers you up when you are sad. And we know a friend is always happy to help. But we just couldn't find one."

Cleo rolled her eyes, but she couldn't help smiling as she said, "A friend is someone to talk to? A friend cheers you up when you are sad? A friend is always happy to help?

You silly, small, scruffy dog! You haven't just found one friend...

you've found lots!"

Pet the Cat

Wes Magee
Illustrated by Pauline Siewert

Pet the Cat

Pet the cat,
   pet the cat
and lift it from the floor.

Pet the cat,
   pet the cat
and shake hands with its paw.

Pet the cat,
   pet the cat
and scratch its head once more.

Pet the cat,
   pet the cat
—then **shoo** it through the door!

In My Yard

There's a cat in my yard
with a wasp on her toes.
    Shake it off,
      shake it off.
Look,
    there
        it
           goes! Buzzzzzzzzzzzzzzzzzzzzz

There's a dog in my yard
with a bee on his nose.
    Shake it off,
      shake it off.
Look,
    there
        it
           goes! Buzzzzzzzzzzzzzzzzz

Recess

Children creeping,
children peeping,
children leaping, leaping, leaping.

Children teasing,
children wheezing,
children sneezing, sneezing, sneezing.

Children calling,
children falling,
children bawling, bawling, bawling.

30

Children hopping,
Children flopping.

There's the bell!

Children,
    children,
        children
            stopping.

Climb the Mountain

Climb the mountain high,
touch the clouds and see the sky.
Feel the wind against you blow,
see the fields far far below.

Animal Chat

Dogs growl,
Wolves howl.
  Cows moo,
  Doves coo.
Lions roar,
Crows caw.
  Horses neigh,
  Donkeys bray.
Monkeys shriek,
Mice squeak.
  Parrots squawk
  ...and I talk.

My Dog's First Poem
(To be read in a dog's voice)

My barking drives them
    up the wall.
I chew the carpet
    in the hall.
I love to chase
    a bouncing...**banana**?

Everywhere I leave
    long hairs.
I fight the cushions
    on the chairs.
Just watch me race
    right up the...**shower**?

Once I chewed
    a piece of chalk.
I get bored when
    the family talk.
Then someone takes me
    for a...**wheelbarrow**?

My Teachers

My teacher's name is Mrs. Large.
She's helped by Mrs. Small.

Miss. Thin comes in
  and she puts up
our paintings
  on the wall.

Big Mr. Bigg's
  the music man.
He's round
  and very tall.

There are
  so **many** teachers,
and I really like
  them all.

Yellow Boots

We're wearing yellow boots
    and the rain has stopped a-thumping.
We're wearing yellow boots
    and now we're puddle jumping!

We're wearing yellow boots
    and the thunder's stopped a-crashing.
We're wearing yellow boots
    and now we're puddle splashing!

Dressing Up

Ben can be a pirate,
and Jade can be a clown.
Jake can be a mailman
walking 'round the town.

Nina can be a princess,
and Mitch can be a knight.
Jess can be a monster
and give us all a **fright**!

Ahmed can be a spaceman,
and Sarah can be a queen.
Jack can be a giant
dressed in red and green.

Jasmine can be a cowgirl,
and Mark can be a king.
Tim can be a wizard
with a magic ring.

Matt can be a doctor,
and Meg can be a nurse.
I will be a teacher
reading out this verse.

Guess Who?

My vest is blue,
   my socks are red.
     A purple hat
       sits on my head.

My shorts are pink,
   my shirt is black.
     Six silver stars
       shine on my back.

My gloves are gold,
   my shoes are brown.
     Who am I?

A circus clown!

39

I'm a Rabbit

I'm a rabbit,
  rolled in a ball.

I'm a horse,
  jumping a wall.

I'm a mouse,
  nibbling at cheese.

I'm a dog,
  scratching its fleas.

I'm a hen,
  pecking at straw.

And I'm a cat,
  asleep on the floor.

The Autumn Leaves

In the autumn
the trees wave in the wind
and the leaves come
tumbling...

down,

down,

down,

down.

Here they come,
hundreds and thousands of leaves
in yellow, red,

hazel,

and

gold,

chocolate brown.

41

A Week of Winter Weather

On Monday icy rain poured down
and flooded streets all over town.

Monday

Tuesday's gales bashed elm and ash,
dead branches came down with a crash.

Tuesday

On Wednesday bursts of hail and sleet.
No one walked along our street.

Wednesday

Thursday stood out clear and calm,
but the sun was paler than my arm.

Thursday

Friday's frost that bit your ears
was cold enough to freeze your tears.

42

Friday

Saturday's sky was ghostly gray.
We smashed ice on the lake today.

Saturday

Christmas Eve was Sunday...and
snow fell like foam across the land.

Sunday

Our Snowman

Wow, fatter and fatter and fatter he grows!
We give him button eyes and a red carrot nose.
He has a thick scarf for the North Wind that blows
and slippers to warm his cold toes,

    his cold toes,

      and slippers to warm
    his cold toes!

Up the Wooden Hill

Yawn!
to bed.
wooden hill
up the
going
sleepyhead,
dreamy
I'm a
Ted.
to one-armed
holding on
to bed,
wooden hill
Up the
Yawn!

Counting to Sleep

One. Two. Three. Four.
Five. Six. And Seven more.
Counting spiders,
counting flies,
counting rabbits,
  close
      your
         eyes...

One. Two. Three. Four.
Five. Six. And Seven more.
Counting horses,
counting sheep,
counting seagulls,
  fall...
     asleep.

45

Little Red Riding Hood

Written by Anne Faundez
Illustrated by Elisa Squillace

Once upon a time, there was a little girl who lived in a village near the woods. Her name was Little Red Riding Hood.

Do you know why she was called Little Red Riding Hood? It was because she had a beautiful red cloak with a hood, specially made by her granny.

The girl was very proud of her cloak
and she wore it all the time. So everyone
called her Little Red Riding Hood.

One day, Little Red Riding Hood's granny was sick in bed. Little Red Riding Hood helped her mother bake a cake for her granny.

"Little Red Riding Hood, take the cake to your granny. Come home before the sun goes down, and don't talk to strangers," said Little Red Riding Hood's mother.

50

Little Red Riding Hood put the cake in a basket and set off for her granny's cottage, on the other side of the woods.

The sun was high in the sky, and sunlight filled the woods. Birds sang in the trees and little creatures bustled to and fro across the path. Little Red Riding Hood was very happy.

In the distance, Little Red Riding Hood saw a glade full of bright blue and pink flowers. She wandered off the path toward them. Granny will love these flowers, she thought. She picked some flowers and then continued on her way. By this time, the sun was low in the sky.

Suddenly, she heard a noise.
A scuffling, shuffling noise.
A big gray wolf stood in front of her.
  "Where are you going?" he asked.
  "I'm going to visit my granny.
She lives on the other
side of the woods and
she's not very well,"
replied Little Red
Riding Hood.

Little Red Riding Hood had forgotten that her mother told her not to speak to strangers.

"I'd like to visit her, too," said the wolf. "You know what? You go your way and I'll take another path." The wolf took a short cut.
Little Red Riding Hood continued on her way.

Now and then, Little Red Riding Hood stopped to pick more flowers. By now, the sun had set and the woods were filled with shadows.

The wolf arrived at Granny's house. He rapped on the door. Knock. Knock.

"Who's there?" asked Granny.

"Little Red Riding Hood," replied the wolf, in a squeaky voice.

"Lift the latch, my dear, and come in," said Granny.

The wolf bounded into the room.
He yanked the old lady out
of bed and bundled her
into a closet.

He jumped into her bed and
pulled the blankets up to his chin.

Little Red Riding Hood arrived at her granny's house. She rapped on the door.
Knock. Knock.
  "Who's there?" said a voice.
  "Little Red Riding Hood," she answered.
  "Lift the latch, my dear, and come in," called the voice.

Now, Little Red Riding Hood had never seen her granny sick in bed. She was surprised.

"Granny, what BIG arms you've got!" she said.

"All the better to hug you with, my dear," said the wolf.

"Granny, what BIG ears you've got!" she said.
 "All the better to hear you with, my dear," said the wolf.
 "Granny, what BIG eyes you've got!" she said.
"All the better to see you with, my dear," said the wolf.

"Granny, what BIG teeth you've got!" she said.
"All the better to **EAT** you with, my dear!"

And the wolf jumped out of bed and chased Little Red Riding Hood around the room.

Just at that moment, by the light of the moon, a woodcutter was passing by. He heard a terrible banging and clanging coming from the cottage. He rushed inside and chased that wicked wolf right out of the woods and far away.

Little Red Riding Hood thanked the woodcutter. Then she unpacked her basket, and Granny, the woodcutter, and Little Red Riding Hood sat down to a feast of cake. And they all lived happily ever after.

The Jolly Rascal

Written by Clare Bevan

Illustrated by Angela Jolliffe

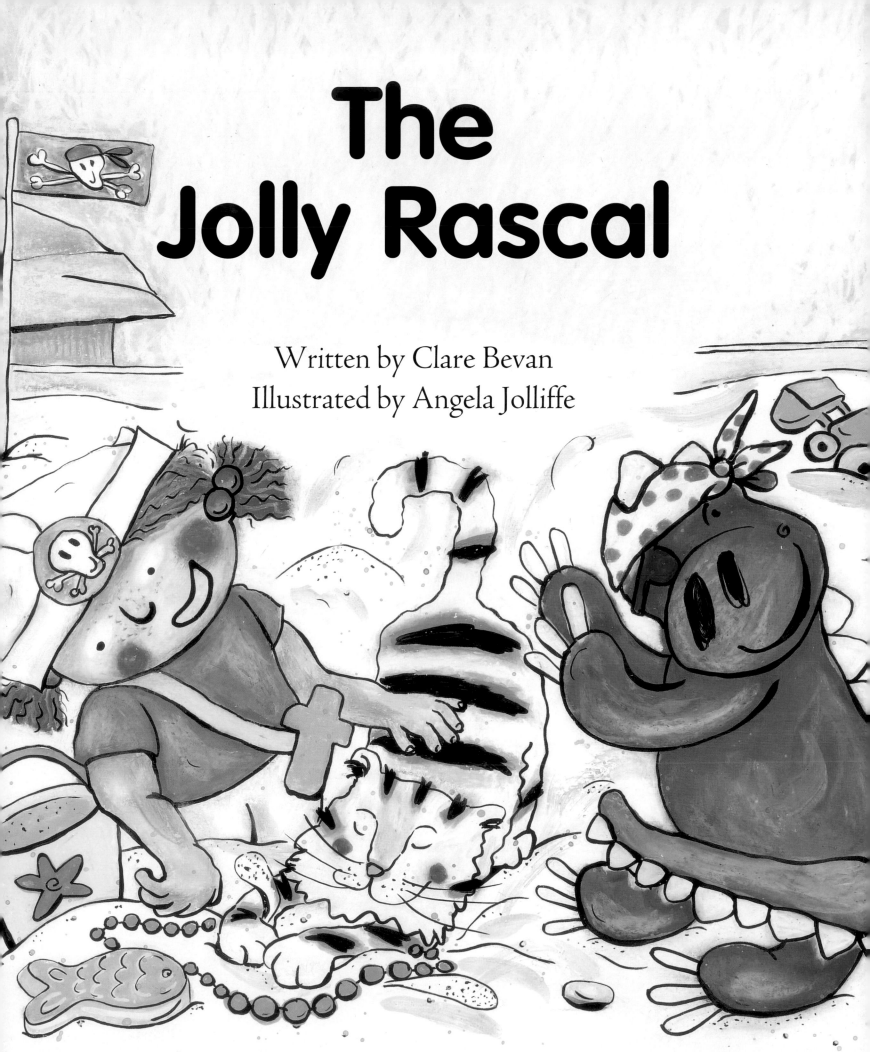

The Jolly Rascal sails away
Across the stormy sea,
With Captain Flo
And Big Bad Joe,
And pirates, one, two, three.

"Land ho! Land ho!"
 says Captain Flo.
"Let's look for gold," says Joe.
They flap, flap, flap
The treasure map,
The pirates say,
 "Let's go!"

They crawl around the rocky ground,
They crawl around the trees
Where monsters peep,
Where tigers creep,
And pirates rub their knees.

"Away we go," says Captain Flo.
"Away we go," says Joe,
"With me and you,
With Tiger, too,
And pirates in a row."

They find a place where rivers race,
Where fishes swim about,
Where waters CRASH,
And ducks go SPLASH!
The pirates say, "Look out!"

They find a bay where people say,
"We're glad you came this way...
Here's food for you
And Tiger, too."
The pirates shout,
    "Hooray!"

"Follow me,"
   says Captain Flo.
"Follow me," says Joe,
"Past hut and hole
   and totem pole."
The pirates shout,
   "Bravo!"

They stamp their feet to a jungle beat,
They find a magic fountain.
Tiger passes
Stripy grasses
And the pirates climb
 a mountain.

"Up we go!" says Captain Flo.
"Up we go!" says Joe,
"Climb so high
We touch the sky."
The pirates peer below.

They all look for
a sandy shore,
They all look at the map...
Across the land
They spot the sand!
The pirates cheer and clap.

Says Flo to Joe,
"Sing yo, ho, ho!
The Jolly Rascal Song.
Dig far, dig low,
Dig fast, dig slow!"
The pirates sing along.

They dig the sand with shovels
    and hands,
At last the treasure's here...
The golden rings,
The shiny things!
The pirates clap and cheer.

81

"Home we go,"
    says Captain Flo.
"Home we go," says Joe,
"With bags of gold
For us to hold."
The pirates sing,
    "Yo, ho!"

The Jolly Rascal sails away
From sand and land and tree,
With Captain Flo
And Big Bad Joe,
And pirates, one, two, three.

So Captain Flo
and Big Bad Joe,
They cross the sea so deep.
In time for tea,
Then happily...
The pirates
fall asleep.

The Wonderful Gift

Written by Clare Bevan

Illustrated by Kelly Waldek

When the little princess was born, the King and Queen were VERY excited.

"She will have EVERYTHING she wants," said the King.

"She will be the happiest princess in the whole world," said the Queen.

They gave her a golden rattle and a teddy bear with soft, silky fur. They rocked her in a silver cradle.

The little princess cried and cried and CRIED.

"Give the little princess a beautiful name," said the Wise Man. "Then she will be happy."
So the King and the Queen looked through a big book and chose the most beautiful name they could find.

"She will be called Princess Starlight," said the Queen. "Her room will be decorated with stars," said the King.

Princess Starlight cried and cried and CRIED.

One year later, Princess Starlight was STILL crying.
"Give her a birthday party," said the Wise Man.
"Everyone will bring her a present.
Then she will be happy."

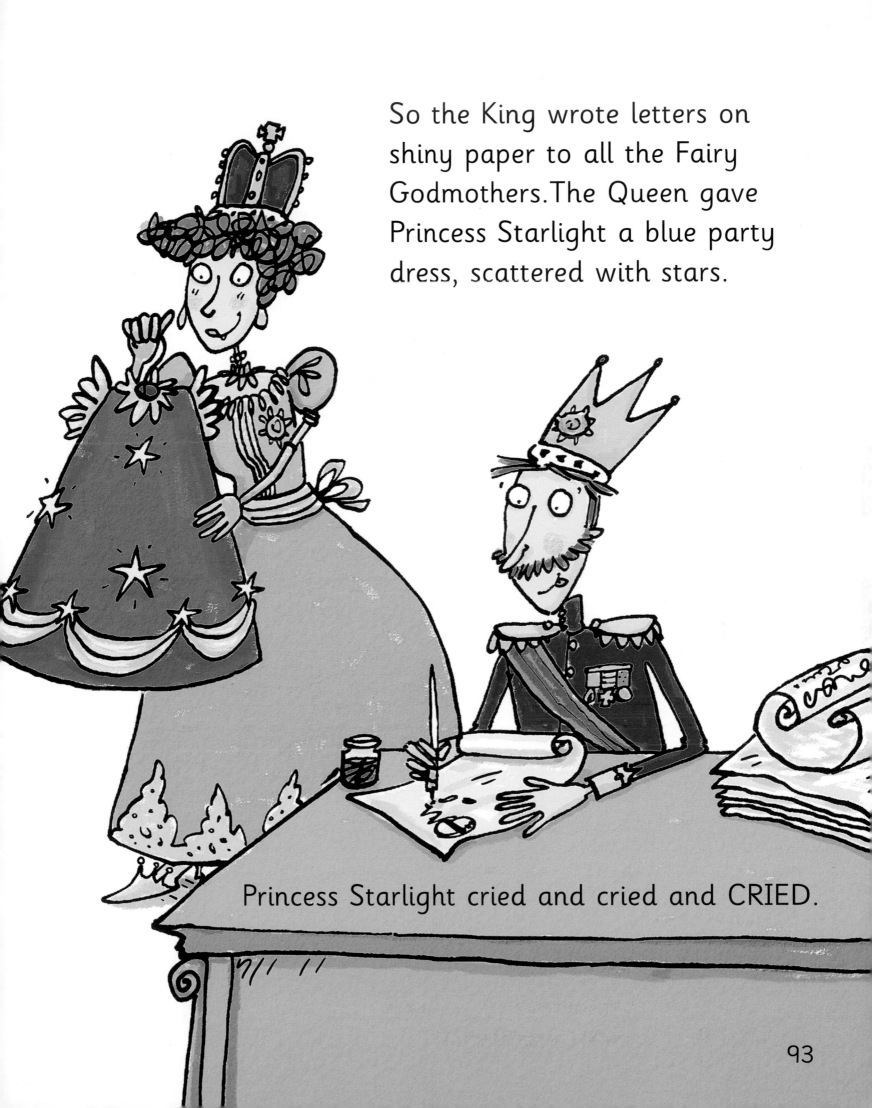

So the King wrote letters on shiny paper to all the Fairy Godmothers. The Queen gave Princess Starlight a blue party dress, scattered with stars.

Princess Starlight cried and cried and CRIED.

It was a very nice party. There was a big
birthday cake with one candle and hundreds
of sugar stars. There were balloons shaped
like stars, and a mountain of presents
wrapped in starry paper.

"Now our little princess will be happy," said the King.
  "Now she will smile," said the Queen.

Princess Starlight looked at her cake and her balloons and her presents. She was quiet for a whole minute.

Then she started to CRY.

The Fairy Godmothers said, "We will give our presents to Princess Starlight. Then she will be happy."

They gave her a tiny flying horse, a talking mirror that could tell jokes, a crown made of moonbeams, and a box of magic jewels.

Princess Starlight looked at
her presents for a long time.
Everyone held their breath.
Then she CRIED.

Many years went by.

Princess Starlight still wore beautiful dresses scattered with stars. Inside her starry room, she kept her magical presents.

Every day, jesters and jugglers tried to make her smile.

Every day, the King and Queen tried to make her happy.

But she STILL felt sad and wanted to cry.

One day, she heard someone singing outside her window. "Who is THAT?" she asked grumpily.

Princess Starlight stomped down the palace stairs to see the King and Queen. "Someone is making an AWFUL noise outside my window," she complained. "You must stop him right now."

"Of course," said the King and Queen. "If it will make you happy."

So the palace policeman found the singer and marched him indoors.

It was the gardener's son.
He looked very grubby,
but he had twinkly eyes.

"Why are you so happy?"
asked Princess Starlight angrily.

The gardener's son smiled. "Because the sun is shining and the flowers are growing," he answered.

"I don't understand," said Princess Starlight with a frown. "I have all my treasures, yet I feel sad."

"That is because you do not have the Wonderful Gift of Happiness," said the gardener's son.

"Where can we find this Wonderful Gift?" asked the King and Queen.

"Princess Starlight must find it for herself," said the gardener's son.

He led Princess Starlight outside and showed her how to dig in the dirt. Together, they planted seeds and sang funny songs. They worked for many weeks.

One day, Princess Starlight ran indoors. She was grubby, but she was smiling and her arms were full of starry flowers.

"I still haven't found the Gift of Happiness," she laughed.

But, of course, she had. Hadn't she?

Katie's Mom is a Mermaid

Written by Hannah Ray
Illustrated by Dawn Vince

There's a new girl in my class,
Her name is Katie Lou,
Her hair is shiny, all golden curls,
Her eyes are sparkly blue.

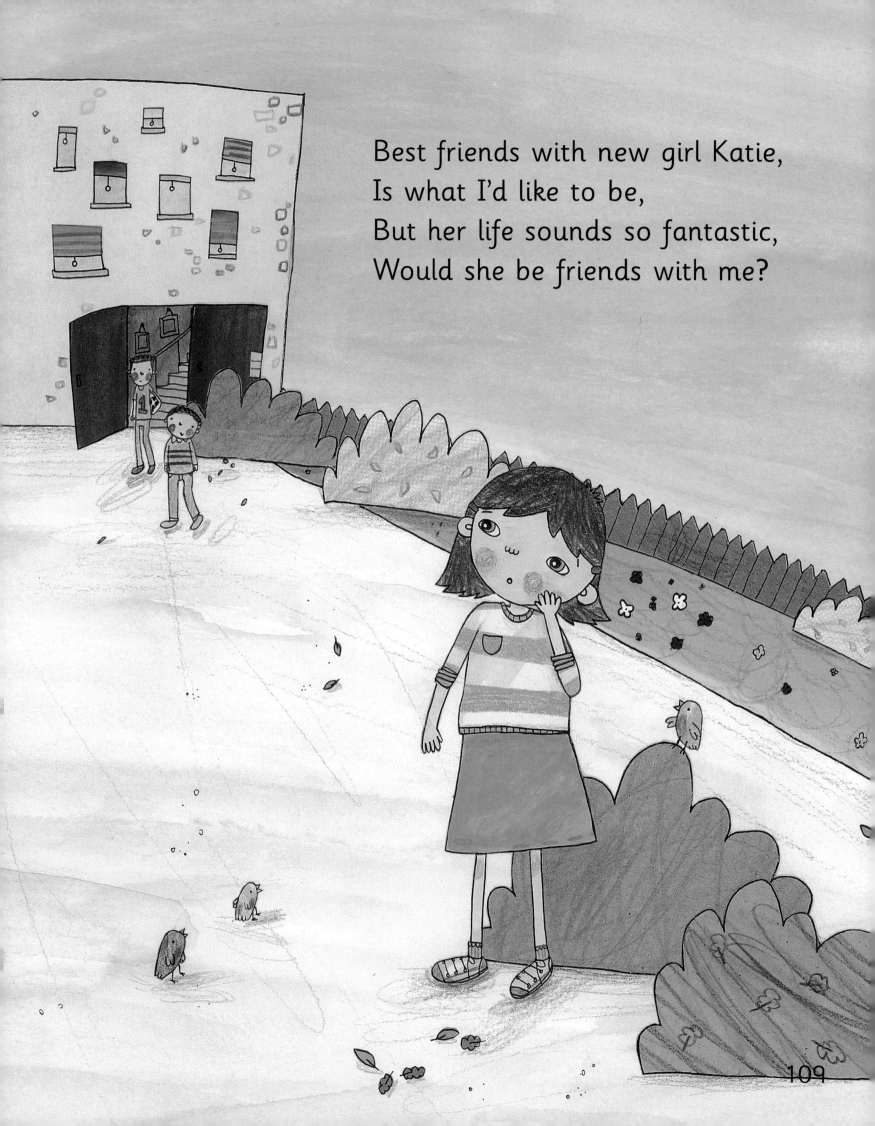

Best friends with new girl Katie,
Is what I'd like to be,
But her life sounds so fantastic,
Would she be friends with me?

109

She says her mom's a mermaid,
Who sings in an ocean band.
An octopus plays the drums,
You can hear him on dry land.

Her dad's a famous cowboy,
Who rides a big white horse.
He gallops through the wild, wild west,
Catching outlaws, of course!

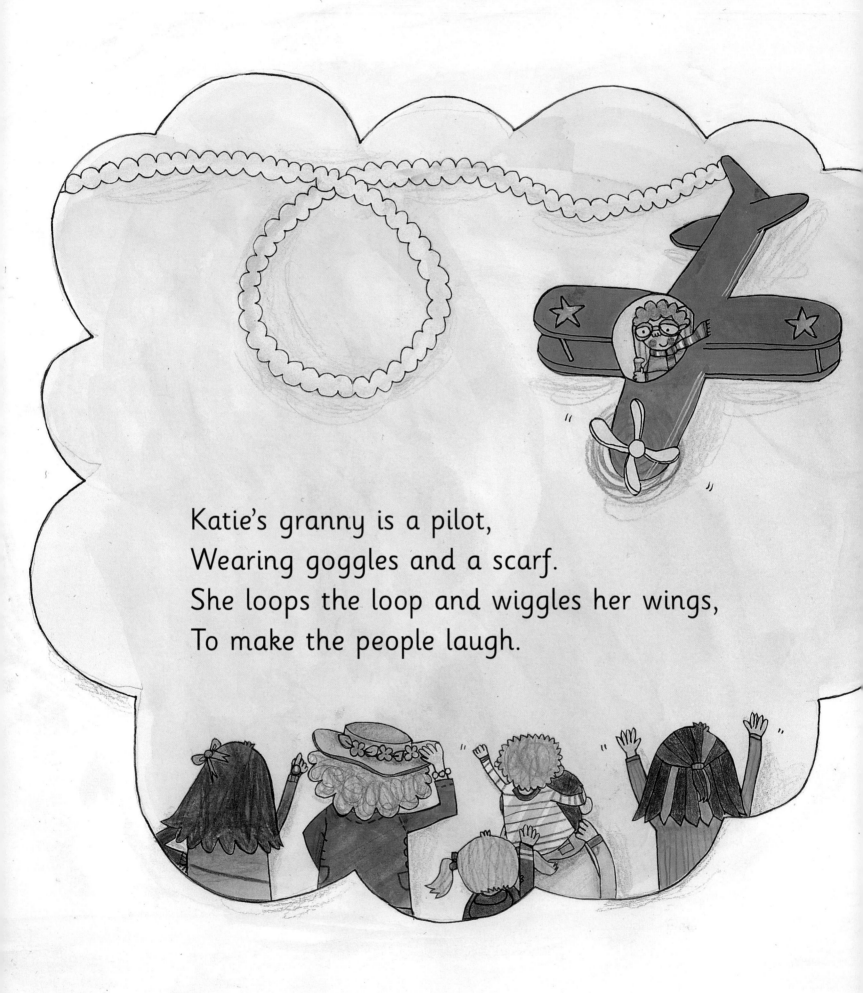

Katie's granny is a pilot,
Wearing goggles and a scarf.
She loops the loop and wiggles her wings,
To make the people laugh.

Her brother is a strongman,
Although he's only three,
Lifting elephants on one hand,
For all the world to see.

Katie's house is a castle,
With a drawbridge and a moat,
She says it gets quite chilly,
So she wears a giant coat.

There are butlers and a gardener,
A driver and a cook,
So grand it is, that Katie says,
A queen came to take a look.

Last Friday Katie asked me,
To go around and play.
But after saying that I would,
She was quiet all day.

Katie led the way back home,
We wandered down the street.
I asked her where the castle was,
But she looked at her feet.

And when we got to Katie's house,
What a big shock I had!
A house like mine, with a bright red door,
Opened by Katie's dad.

A regular guy, not a cowboy,
Her dad delivers mail.
And Katie's mom, I soon found out,
Has legs and not a tail.

Katie's brother played with toys,
He showed me his best bear.
And her granny was just like mine,
Though she did have bright pink hair!

But Katie still looked worried,
"I'm very sorry," she said.
She looked like she might start to cry,
Her face was very red.

Katie said, in a tiny voice,
"I told a fib or two,
But I wanted you to like me,
It's hard being brand new!"

But I am just like Katie,
I love to play pretend,
And now we are two princesses,
And are the best of friends!

Tiddalik the Frog

Written by Anne Faundez

Illustrated by Sanja Rescek

Long ago, in the Dreamtime, a huge red frog roamed the earth. His name was Tiddalik.

Tiddalik was so large that his back touched the sky. He was so wide that he filled the space between two mountain ranges. When he moved, the ground trembled and his feet made holes as big as valleys.

One day, he woke up from a very bad sleep.
He was VERY, VERY grumpy!
He was also VERY, VERY thirsty!

"Water! Water!" he bellowed.
His words made the clouds crackle with thunder.

He found a river and drank up all the water.
He found a lake and emptied that, too.
He kept on drinking until every waterhole was dry.

Tiddalik was now bulging with water and ready to burst.

He was too uncomfortable to move. He shut his eyes and fell into a long, deep sleep.

The days went by.

Tiddalik slept.

There was no sign
of rain in the skies.

The sun scorched
the earth. The
grasses withered
and the trees lost
their leaves.

The beautiful green
earth became hard
and cracked.

131

Kangaroo, Kookaburra, and Platypus
were anxious. They had watched
Tiddalik drinking up all the water.
Now their land was turning to dust.

"The earth is so cracked that I can't hop around anymore," grumbled Kangaroo.

"There's nowhere for me to swim," moaned Platypus.

"Tiddalik MUST return our water!" said Kookaburra.

But the animals were scared to talk to Tiddalik. He was still so grumpy!

"I know," said Kookaburra.
"Let's make him laugh. Then
he'll spill out the water."

So Kookaburra flew right up to
Tiddalik. She sang some funny
songs. She wiggled and jiggled
and danced around.

Tiddalik opened one eye.
He shut it again.

Platypus went up to Tiddalik. She told a
few jokes and then she flipped and flopped
and shuffled around.

Tiddalik opened the other eye.
He shut it again.

Next, it was Kangaroo's turn.
He loved to show off.
He twirled and whirled,
and thumped and
bumped his tail around.

Tiddalik opened both eyes.
He shut them again.
He was still bored.

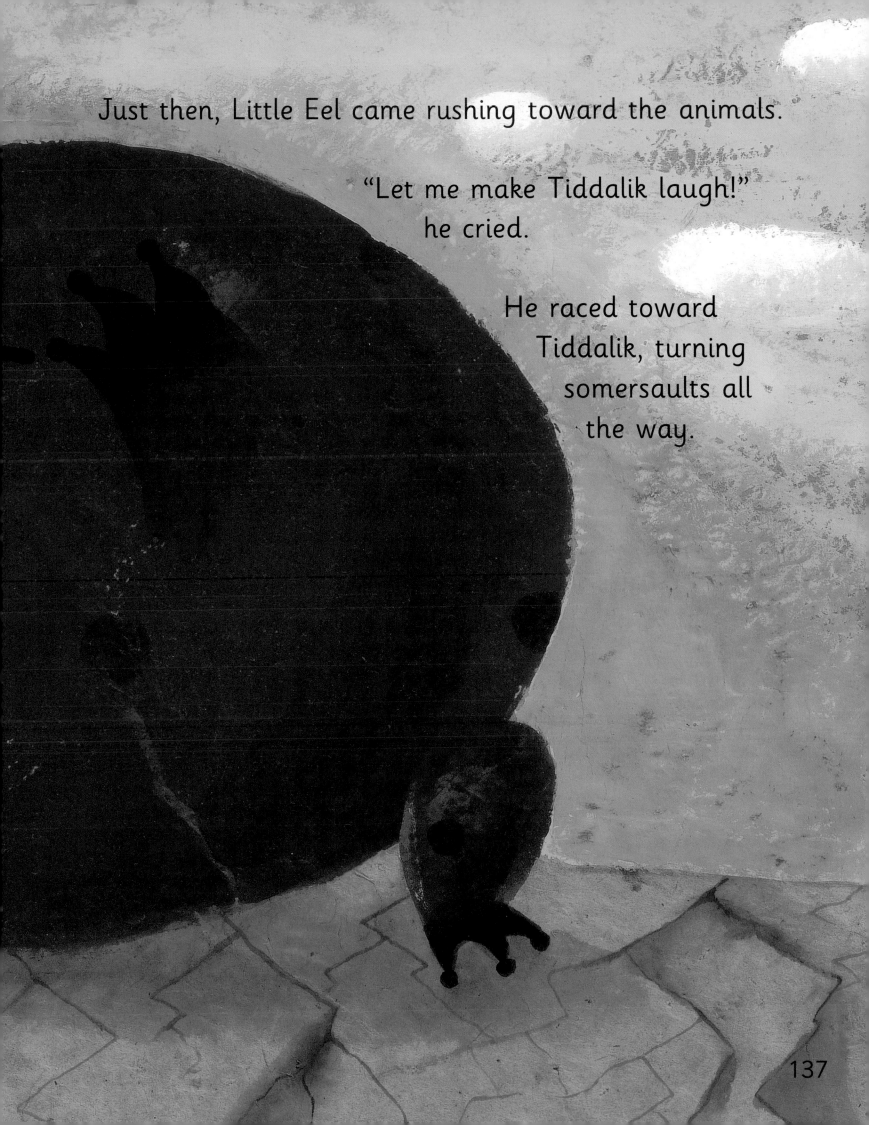

Just then, Little Eel came rushing toward the animals.

"Let me make Tiddalik laugh!" he cried.

He raced toward Tiddalik, turning somersaults all the way.

Little Eel landed on Tiddalik's bulging stomach.
He scrambled to get himself upright.
He teetered and tottered and then stood,
looking up at the gigantic frog.

Tiddalik opened his eyes. He was
so astonished to see Little Eel,
all shivering and shaking,
sitting right on his belly.

Tiddalik made a rumbling noise.
He chuckled—and a trickle of water
dribbled from his mouth.

He chuckled some more.

Soon, he was rumbling with laughter.
Water spilled from his mouth and ran down his sides.
Tiddalik couldn't stop laughing at the sight of
Little Eel sitting on his belly.
As he laughed, he felt less grumpy.

Soon, the land was awash with water.
The grasses began to grow again, and tiny leaves
began to cover the bare branches of the trees.

And do you know what? To this day, Tiddalik
has never again emptied the land of water.
Why?

Well, Little Eel knows just what to do now when Tiddalik gets grumpy...and thirsty!

Ready for a Picnic

Written by Celia Warren
Illustrated by Elke Zinsmeister

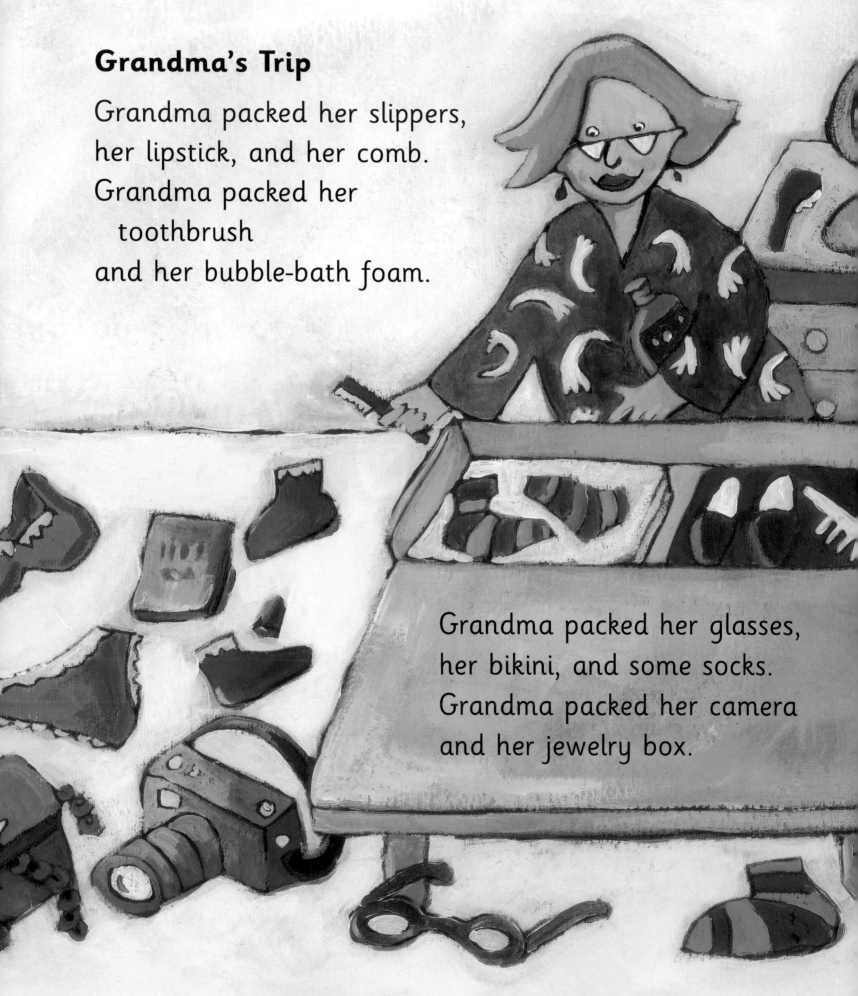

Grandma's Trip

Grandma packed her slippers,
her lipstick, and her comb.
Grandma packed her
   toothbrush
and her bubble-bath foam.

Grandma packed her glasses,
her bikini, and some socks.
Grandma packed her camera
and her jewelry box.

Grandma packed her folding chair,
and all her bags,
then, last of all, before she left,
Grandma packed...Gramps!

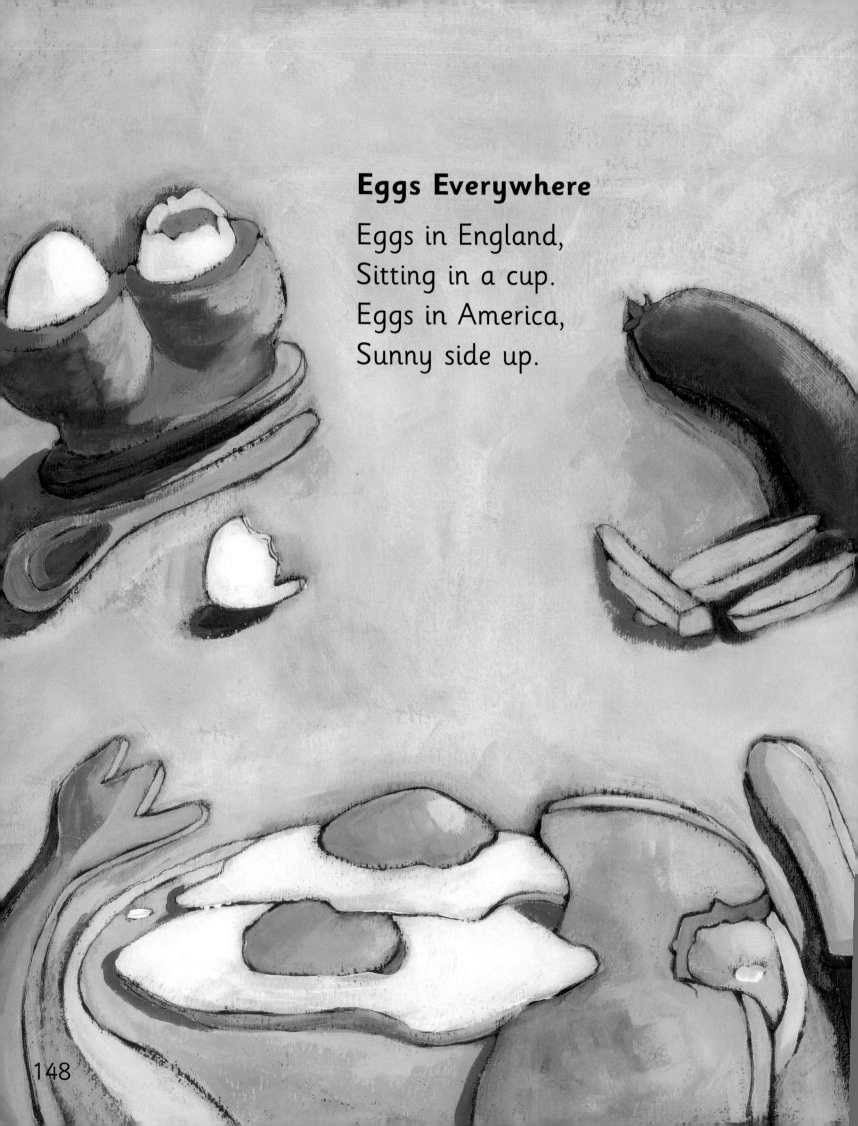

Eggs Everywhere

Eggs in England,
Sitting in a cup.
Eggs in America,
Sunny side up.

Ready for a Picnic

One for a sandwich,
Two for a cake,
Three for some ice cream by the lake.

Four for an apple,
Five for a pear,
Six for a picnic—
    see you there!

The Dizzy Hamster

"Tell me, little hamster, how does it feel
going 'round and 'round in your little wheel?"

"Well," said the hamster, "what I have found
is when the wheel stops, then the room goes 'round."

Giraffe

I'd like my head to be
   up in the blue,
Giraffe, giraffe, I'd like to be you.

I'd like to be as tall as a tree,
Giraffe, giraffe, would you
   like to be me?

I like the way you make
   funny faces,
Giraffe, giraffe, would you
   like to change places?

What Can I Be?

I can be a penguin and waddle as I walk,
I can be a parrot with a funny way to talk,
I can be a hamster and curl up small,
I can be a dog and bring you a ball,
I can be a monkey and swing from a tree
But, if it's okay, I can just be me.

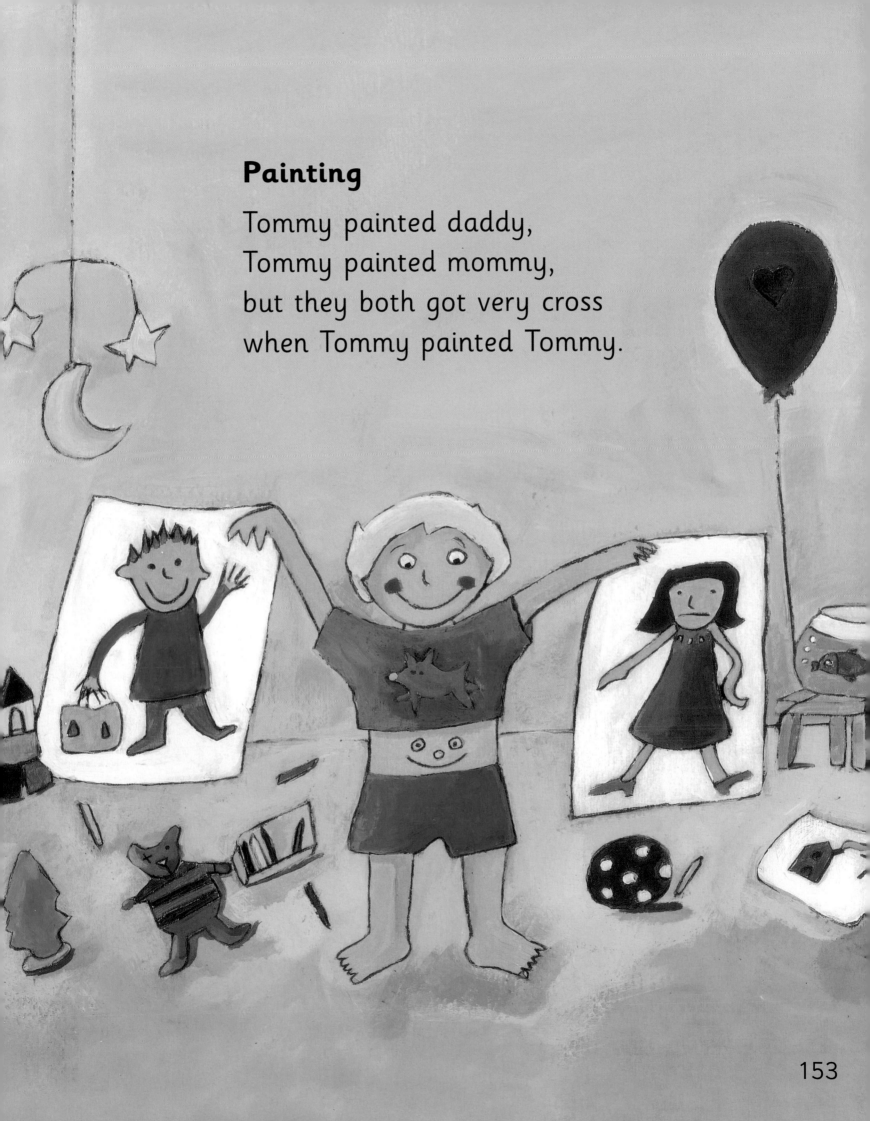

Painting

Tommy painted daddy,
Tommy painted mommy,
but they both got very cross
when Tommy painted Tommy.

Off We Go

Up the hill

By the waterfall, then...

Over the wall,

Tumbling, turning

Down the road,

All the way down

Hats

Paper hats for parties,
Flowered hats for show,
Sun hats in summer,
Everywhere you go.

Hard hats for bricklayers,
A white hat for a cook,
Stocking caps in winter,
Everywhere you look.

Riddles

The shape
of a plate or a
coin, the full moon
or a bowl of soup, the
shape of a button, the
sun or a wheel, what
shape is as round
as a hoop?

A
roof
or the shape
of the ear of a cat,
three sides and three
corners, what shape is that?

Landscape

My potato is an island.
The gravy is the sea.
The peas are people swimming.
The biggest one is me.

My carrots are whales
That make the sea wavy
But the big, brown blobs
Are LUMPS in the gravy!

Washing the Dishes

Knives and forks and spoons in a jumble,
Dishes clatter, splash, and tumble,
Bubbles in the sink where fingers fumble,
Doing the dishes.
SPLASH!

Ten Bold Pirates

Ten bold pirates,
   all shipshape,
Two got seasick
   and that left eight.

Eight bold pirates
   playing tricks,
Two met a shark
   and that left six.

Six bold pirates,
   tired of being poor,
Two found treasure
   and that left four.

Four bold pirates
   feeling blue,
Two swam home again
   and that left two.

Two bold pirates
   drinking rum,
They fell asleep
   and that left none.

Index